The Night Before
MOTHERS DAY

Grosset & Dunlap
An Imprint of Penguin Group (USA) Inc.

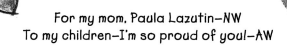

For my mom, Paula Lazutin–NW
To my children–I'm so proud of you!–AW

GROSSET & DUNLAP
Published by the Penguin Group
Penguin Group (USA) Inc., 375 Hudson Street, New York, New York 10014, USA
Penguin Group (Canada), 90 Eglinton Avenue East, Suite 700,
Toronto, Ontario M4P 2Y3, Canada
(a division of Pearson Penguin Canada Inc.)
Penguin Books Ltd, 80 Strand, London WC2R 0RL, England
Penguin Ireland, 25 St Stephen's Green, Dublin 2, Ireland
(a division of Penguin Books Ltd)
Penguin Group (Australia), 707 Collins Street, Melbourne, Victoria 3008, Australia
(a division of Pearson Australia Group Pty Ltd)
Penguin Books India Pvt Ltd, 11 Community Centre,
Panchsheel Park, New Delhi–110 017, India
Penguin Group (NZ), 67 Apollo Drive, Rosedale, Auckland 0632, New Zealand
(a division of Pearson New Zealand Ltd)
Penguin Books (South Africa), Rosebank Office Park,
181 Jan Smuts Avenue, Parktown North 2193, South Africa
Penguin China, B7 Jiaming Center, 27 East Third Ring Road North,
Chaoyang District, Beijing 100020, China

Penguin Books Ltd, Registered Offices: 80 Strand, London WC2R 0RL, England

Text copyright © 2010 by Natasha Wing. Illustrations copyright © 2010 Penguin Group (USA) Inc. All rights reserved.
Published by Grosset & Dunlap, a division of Penguin Young Readers Group, 345 Hudson Street, New York, New York 10014.
GROSSET &DUNLAP is a trademark of Penguin Group (USA) Inc. Printed in China.

Library of Congress Control Number: 2009006073

ISBN 978-0-448-45213-5   10 9 8

The Night Before
MOTHER'S DAY

We ♥ Mom

By Natasha Wing • Illustrated by Amy Wummer

Grosset & Dunlap
An Imprint of Penguin Group (USA) Inc.

'Twas the night before Mother's Day
when, as quiet as a mouse,
Dad told us his plan
to get Mom out of the house.

Her sneakers were set by the doorway with care

in hopes that her running pals soon would be there.

Then out in the yard
there arose quite a crowd.

"Come on! Let's go, girl!"
her friends shouted real loud.

So Mom in her sweat suit and red baseball cap
plugged in her earphones . . .

and *jogged* off in a snap.

Away to the kitchen we flew like a flash

as if we were running a one-hundred-yard dash!

We measured and mixed
a delicious cake batter,

then blended the frosting—oops!
Way too much splatter!

We made fancy cards
adding our "I Love Yous,"

and a special coupon
that Mom sure could use.

When Mom came home, she saw the mess in the sink.

"What'd I miss?"
she asked.
"Nothing," Dad said
with a wink.

We children then nestled
all snug in our beds,
while visions of Mom
danced in our heads.

The next morning we presented a giant bouquet.

"It's for you, Mom!" we cried. "Happy Mother's Day!"

She read both of our cards and, after wiping her eyes, said, "A private spa session! What a lovely surprise."

MOM

I ♥ MOM

We took Mom to the kitchen where our spa was set up. Dad served her black coffee in an extra large cup.

We rubbed her shoulders.
We massaged her feet.
Mom sighed and smiled.
"You kids are so sweet."

I wrapped a towel turban
to cover her hair,
then we dabbed on a mud mask.
No mess anywhere!

I painted her nails.
What glittery fun!
A top coat of polish—
voilà! Manicure done!

Dad said, "The chef will be serving a divine gourmet brunch."
(That's a meal that comes between breakfast and lunch.)

So Mom hurried off
to go and get dressed.
We took seats at the table,
behaving our best.

When what to our wondering eyes should appear—
but the perfect model for Mother of the Year!

Her eyes—
how they sparkled!
Her brown hair—
how curly!
Her cheeks were
like roses,
her skirt—
very twirly!

We raised our juice glasses
and offered a toast:
"To the World's Greatest Mom
And that's not a boast."

Mom thanked us for everything—
it brought her such cheer.
She wished it could be Mother's Day
every day of the year.